THE MYSTERY
ON THE
Great
Lakes

3

Managing Editor: Sherry Moss
Assistant Editor: Christina Barber
Cover Design: Vicki DeJoy
Content Design: Randolyn Friedlander

Gallopade International is introducing SAT words that kids need to know in
each new book that we publish. The SAT words are bold in the story. Look
for this special logo beside each word in the glossary. Happy Learning!

Gallopade is proud to be a member and supporter of these educational organizations
and associations:

American Booksellers Association
American Library Association
International Reading Association
National Association for Gifted Children
The National School Supply and Equipment Association
The National Council for the Social Studies
Museum Store Association
Association of Partners for Public Lands
Association of Booksellers for Children
Association for the Study of African American Life and History
National Alliance of Black School Educators

Once upon a time…

Hmm, kids keep asking me to write a mystery book. What shall I do?

Mimi

Write one about spiders!

You two really are characters, that's all I've got to say!

Yes you are! And, of course I choose you! But what should I write about?

 National Parks!

 *SCARY PLACES!*

Famous Places!

FUN PLACES!

Disney World!

New York City!

Dracula's Castle

GRAND CANYON

On the *Mystery Girl* airplane ...

I Can FLY US anYWHeRe!

Mystery Girl

Or aboard
the *Mimi!*

Mimi

Take me to the
Forbidden City!

Or by surfboard,
rickshaw,
motorbike,
camel ...

All great ideas!
I can put a lot of history,
MYSTERY,
legend, lore, and laughs in
the books! We can use other boys and girls
in the books. It will be educational and fun!

Good
stuff!

And so, Mimi, Papa, Christina, and Grant took off aboard the *Mystery Girl* and America's National Mystery Book Series—where the adventure is real and so are the characters!—was born.

START YOUR ADVENTURE TODAY!

READ THE BOOK!

GO ONLINE!

TRACK YOUR ADVENTURES!

APPLY TO BE A CHARACTER!

Yikes! That was close!

Rats!

What I Did on My Vacation

by Grant

We went to the Great Lakes. It was great! If you don't know where they are, well, they are across the top of the United States, on the border between us and Canada. If you don't know how to remember the Great Lakes, just think: HOMES–Huron, Ontario, Michigan, Erie, and Superior. The Great Lakes are so gigantic that you really can't see from one side to another. They really seem more like oceans, especially on stormy days.

I went from one lake to the other on a big adventure with my sister, Christina, and my grandparents, Mimi and Papa. We even met new friends–and a villain–along the way. I learned a lot about shipwrecks, sand dunes, and scary stuff like haunted lighthouses. The Great Lakes have a LOT of lighthouses. I'm not sure how much good they do, because the Great Lakes also have a lot of shipwrecks. A LOT of shipwrecks!

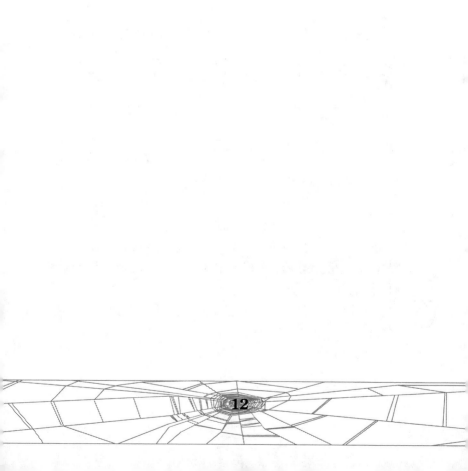

1
WHEN BUFFALOES FLY

Christina wiped her mouth with a bright yellow napkin. The spicy hot sauce from the Buffalo wings stung her lips and tickled her tongue. Her blue eyes watered until tears streaked her cheeks.

Grant grinned, his mouth coated with greasy orange sauce. "These are great! But I didn't know buffaloes had wings." Buffalo sauce covered his hands and trickled down his arms to his elbows.

"Eww, Grant," Christina said. She handed him a napkin.

Mimi laughed. "Glad you like them," she said, "but buffaloes don't have wings. Buffalo wings are chicken. They're named

Buffalo wings because they were invented right here, in Buffalo, New York!"

Even eating the messy Buffalo wings, Mimi kept her white ruffled blouse and red suit jacket spotless. She somehow didn't seem bothered by the super-spicy hot sauce either.

Papa took several long gulps of lemonade. He'd ordered the hottest hot wings, and from the look on his face, they were fiery hot! Of course, Mimi always said he had a mouth made of stainless steel. He could eat—and enjoy—even hot jalapeño peppers.

"Papa, when are we going to the Rock and Roll Hall of Fame?" Christina asked.

"We'll be there in no time," Papa replied, his voice hoarse from the hot sauce. "We're just about ready to kick off our tour of the Great Lakes!"

Grant and Christina often traveled with their mystery-writing grandmother, Mimi, as she did research for her books. Her latest book was to be set on the Great Lakes. Their grandfather, Papa, flew the family wherever they needed to go in his red-and-white airplane, the *Mystery Girl*. Mimi affectionately referred to him as the "cowboy pilot" in his Stetson hat, jeans, and leather boots.

"Once we finish lunch," he explained, "we're off to board the *Mystery Girl*. She'll take us over to Cleveland, Ohio, and can you guess which of the Great Lakes you'll find there?"

"Lake Erie! Right, Papa?" Christina asked.

"That's right." Papa replied.

"*Eeeeerie*?? That's a creepy name for a lake. Then, where were we earlier today?" Grant asked.

"Lake Ontario. Don't you remember, Grant?" Christina said, as she pulled out a map of the Great Lakes and pointed to Lake Ontario. "See, Papa said our route would be Lake Ontario, first. Then Lake Erie, Lake Huron, Lake Superior, and finally Lake Michigan, or vice versa, I forget."

Grant took the map from Christina to get a better look at the route.

Just then, Christina felt the hair on the back of her neck stand up straight. She involuntarily smoothed the hair back in place and turned slowly around in her chair. A family of three sat quietly in the corner of the restaurant. Christina prided herself on her keen observation skills. It baffled her that somehow this family could have passed by their table without her noticing.

A young girl about Christina's age suddenly met her gaze. It made Christina jump a little. The girl's eyes were a striking green. Then, just as quickly, the girl shifted her attention back to her plate. Her simple black dress and tightly pulled back blonde hair made Christina think they were locals. *This family couldn't be on vacation. Why did the girl look so serious? And that boy, too?* He had to be about Grant's age. The boy's dress pants and white button down shirt were just as formal as the girl's clothing.

Papa cleared his throat. "Wasn't it, Christina?"

Christina swung around. "Wasn't it what? Oh, sorry, Papa."

"Niagara Falls. It sure was pretty this morning." He wiped a bead of sweat from his brow, still feeling the effects of the hot sauce. He grabbed his cowboy hat and fanned his face.

Mimi nodded, a tiny smear of sauce on her chin.

"I loved every bit of it!" Christina answered truthfully. "Especially the stories you told us of those daredevils going down the falls in wooden barrels! Just seeing the falls made me wonder why anyone in their right mind would want to do something so crazy!"

"Oh, yeah, that was so cool!" Grant agreed. "I also liked seeing the rainbow over the falls and getting wet from the mist! So, Mimi," Grant continued, "what makes the Great Lakes so, well, great?"

"Well, where do I start?" Mimi said. "One of the main things you should know is that the Great Lakes hold about 20 percent of the fresh surface water in the world!"

Grant looked puzzled. "Fresh water," Mimi explained, "is water on the earth that is not sea water from the ocean. It's found in lakes, rivers, streams...places like that. It's very important for the survival of people and animals on the earth."

DING! A text message arrived on Mimi's cell phone. "I wonder who that could be?" she said, and peered at her bright red phone.

"Oh, it's Ichabod, the lighthouse keeper!" Mimi read the message to herself. She frowned. "Hmm, he seems a bit worried about the lighthouse. Something about odd noises in the night. Not like him. I hope he's okay. He's getting older. I'm not sure how much longer he can traipse up and down those lighthouse steps."

Christina and Grant stopped eating and turned their attention to Mimi.

Mimi snapped her phone shut. "Well, we're set to go see him. He can't wait to meet you two!" she said with a smile.

Grant elbowed Christina. She leaned in and he whispered, "*Ichabod.* That's a creepy name. Sort of like that Headless Horseman dude?"

"Sure is creepy," Christina agreed.

Grant shook his head, bouncing his blonde curls all around. "Sounds almost ...*icky*," he said, scrunching his face.

Christina nodded. "And what about him hearing odd noises? I'm not sure I want to meet Mr. Ichabod after all. Or visit his haunted lighthouse."

Christina hadn't really wanted to go on this trip to the Great Lakes with Mimi and Papa. Even though the fall leaves were spectacular hues of red, yellow, and orange, Christina wished they'd come in the summer so she could swim and not in the fall, when it was too cold to go in the water.

Papa paid the bill and they left the restaurant, but not before Christina stole a quick peek back inside. The family was gone! A young couple was being seated. Christina couldn't help but feel that she had lost an opportunity—but for what, she didn't quite know. Soon, they were aboard the *Mystery Girl*.

"Where are we going now?" Grant asked.

"To Cleveland, Ohio, and Lake Erie," Papa replied.

"And the Rock and Roll Hall of Fame!" Christina added. She was a true rock and roll music lover. She couldn't wait to see all the guitars on display.

"So, we're not going to see Mr. Icky?" Grant asked.

Papa laughed. "Do you mean Mr. Ichabod?"

"Oops, yeah, Mr. Ichabod. Sorry, Papa," Grant said.

"We'll see him later in the trip, Grant," Mimi said.

"Let's get this plane up in the air! Let's rock and roll!" Papa cried, and the *Mystery Girl* launched into the crisp, bright blue autumn sky.

Grant played air guitar in his seat, bounding from side to side. At the end of his animated guitar solo, Grant shouted in his best Elvis Presley impersonation, "Thank you! Thank you very much!"

He bowed to the pretend crowd that had formed to hear him play, flinging his arms to the side. WHACK! He accidentally hit Christina's shoulder.

"Ouch! Quit it, Grant!" Christina cried.

DING! DING! A text message suddenly appeared on Christina's cell phone. *Who could that be from*, she thought. Her eyes grew wide when she opened her phone to read it.

The text message read,

```
BEWARE OF BESSIE, THE
EERIE MONSTER!
```

Christina immediately nudged Grant. "Look at this!" she whispered.

"Who is that from?" Grant asked.

Christina looked a second time at the message. There was no signature or phone number.

"I don't know," she replied and shrugged. "It doesn't say."

Goose bumps rose on Grant's arm. His big blue eyes grew wide with concern. "Maybe it's the Erie monster?"

Christina felt a chill, and pulled her sweater around her. "I sure hope not, because that's exactly where we're headed!"

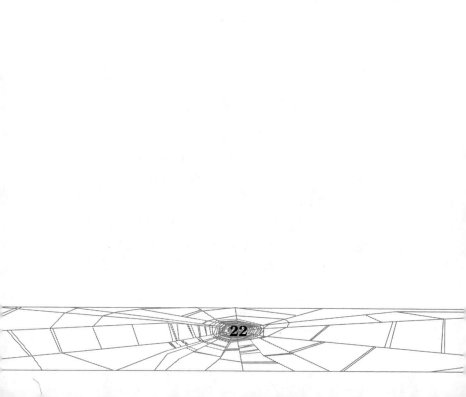

22

2
TOO EERIE

Papa landed the *Mystery Girl* just outside Cleveland, Ohio, on a small airstrip.

As Papa taxied the plane to the red brick terminal building, Grant peered outside. "Hey, there's Papa's SUV," he remarked.

"And she's got the boat *Mimi* hooked up behind her and ready to go with us," Papa said.

"Are we actually going to go boating on the lakes?" Christina asked. "I thought they were big and rough, even dangerous, this time of year."

"Of course, we are!" Mimi said. "There's a lot to see on the waters of the Great Lakes, like lighthouses, sunken ships, and islands," Mimi said. "And besides," she added, the weather is supposed to be nice and the seas calm."

"Okay, everyone into the SUV. We're heading to the hotel," Papa said.

"But I thought we were going to the see the Rock and Roll Hall of Fame!" Christina moaned.

"We are, but in the morning," Mimi replied, rummaging around in her floppy purse for some red lipstick.

Papa looked at his watch. "And judging from the time, we'd better get a move on if we want to get to our hotel before dark."

Grant and Christina piled into the back of Papa's big grey SUV. Mimi stepped up onto the sideboard in her spiky red heels and joined Papa in the front seat.

Christina didn't want to spend the night in a hotel. She wanted to go see all the interesting things in the Rock and Roll Hall of Fame. She knew there would be guitars and wild and crazy clothes that the stars had worn. But most of all, Christina wanted to hear some music, specifically from her favorite bands, which were, well, ALL OF THEM!

Mimi was already busy at work, making notes, and cooking up her next mystifying plot. She pushed her gem-studded reading glasses up into her blonde hair.

Christina kept trying to picture an island on a lake, but all she kept seeing in her mind were tiny patches of land that one person could barely stand on. It didn't seem quite right that there could be islands on a lake. Christina had visited many different islands with Mimi and Papa on their other trips, but those islands were in the ocean, not in a lake!

Grant kept thinking about the mysterious text message on Christina's phone. He started worrying that some monster in the lake would eat them—and the boat!

As Papa drove around a bend in the road, they all caught their first glimpse of Lake Erie. The enormous expanse of water shimmered in the late afternoon sunlight.

Christina gasped. The lake was huge, and definitely not what she had pictured.

"Papa, I thought you said this was a lake!" she exclaimed.

"It IS a lake, Christina," Papa said.

"But it looks like an OCEAN!" Christina cried.

"It sure is big," agreed Grant.

"Lake Erie is one of the smaller of the Great Lakes," Mimi said. "Lake Ontario, where we just came from, is the smallest. Erie is the second smallest of the Great Lakes."

"How many lakes ARE there?" Grant asked.

"There are five Great Lakes: Ontario, Erie, Michigan, Huron, and Superior," Papa stated. "Just think HOMES and you'll always be able to remember them!"

"If this is small, I can't wait to see the bigger ones!" Grant shouted.

Christina stared out at the vast waters of Lake Erie. She started to worry about being in the little *Mimi* boat out on that huge lake. Upon closer inspection, Christina noticed that the lake actually had waves and whitecaps spitting spindrift. *Now I'm really worried*, she thought.

"Looks like we got here just in time," Papa said, his voice stern. "There's a storm coming in."

Christina and Grant looked at the sky through the car's tinted windows. Dark clouds billowed high into the air. A flash of lightning lit up the bottom of one of the clouds, and the smell of rain filled the air.

As soon as Papa parked the SUV at the hotel, Christina and Grant slid out of the backseat onto the pavement. THUMP!

"Everyone, grab a bag!" Papa yelled. He had a twinkle in his eyes. "Let's see if we can beat the storm."

"HA!" Grant yelled. "That storm's got nothing on me. I'm the fastest bag carrier around." He grabbed one suitcase and Mimi's red checkerboard overnight bag and bolted off toward the hotel entrance.

"Are not!" Christina said, and added, "I am." She grabbed two suitcases and ran after her brother.

She gritted her teeth and chased after Grant. "No fair!" she shouted. "You had a head start!"

Mimi and Papa followed close behind. CLICK! CLACK! Mimi's red heels announced her entrance to the cobblestone-floored hotel lobby.

CRACK! Just as they made it to the safety of the hotel awning, a lightning bolt struck the lake, causing a tremendous flash.

"Whoa!" Grant said.

"Just in time," Mimi added.

"A little rain won't spoil the trip," Papa said. "We'll be out on that lake in the *Mimi* in no time flat. We'll ride those waves like a bucking bronco!" he shouted.

"Yee-haw!" Grant yelled, and started galloping like a horse. Mimi's overnight bag swung to and fro around his neck.

The thought of being in a small boat, riding the waves like a bucking bronco, made Christina's stomach churn. Up and down, up and down. Just the thought of it made her feel seasick.

To squash the sick feeling in her stomach, Christina turned her focus to the lake outside. Mimi and Papa chatted with a desk clerk as he checked them into the hotel.

Grant suddenly appeared next to Christina. He whacked her in the leg with Mimi's still-swinging overnight bag. "What's THAT?" Grant shouted.

Grant's voice startled Christina, and she jumped. "What?" she cried.

"THAT!" Grant pointed, his finger trembling. His face was white.

In the middle of the lake, something bobbed up and down. Christina squinted to get a better look.

Grant shouted, "It's the lake MONSTER!"

3
TRUTH OR MONSTER?

Christina dropped her bags and stepped on the metal grate to keep the hotel's glass doors from sliding closed. Wind and debris blew into the hotel lobby. She couldn't believe her eyes!

Grant stood, frozen with fear, his finger still pointing out at the bobbing thing in the lake.

Papa sidled up next to Grant and Christina. "Well, now if that don't beat all," he said.

Christina looked over at Papa. "What is it, Papa?"

"I believe that's a shipwreck," he replied.

"A shipwreck?" Christina and Grant shouted simultaneously.

"Sure is," Papa said. "There are lots of shipwrecks here in the lakes. These waters can be very dangerous, especially in the winter. Storms have been known to come up out of nowhere, swallow ships right up, and take them to their watery grave."

Christina shivered. She picked up her bags and backed off the grate. The glass doors closed. There, in the reflection of the glass, stood a girl and a boy standing side by side, both in formal clothing.

Christina swung around to see if what she saw was real. But in the process, she bumped into Grant, sending him clear off his feet and into a pile of suitcases. He rolled off of them with a THUMP!

"Oh, are you okay?" The girl and boy said. They had run over to Grant's rescue. They gently helped him up.

"Um, I think. Thanks." Grant stood up.

"Hi," Christina said. "Thanks for helping my brother. I'm Christina. And this is my brother, Grant."

The girl smiled. "Hi, I'm Nicole," she said. "This is my brother, Dominic."

"I remember you two from the restaurant in Buffalo," Christina said.

"Me too," Nicole answered.

"I'm sorry I was staring. It's just that you, well, seemed a little..."

"...out of place?" Nicole finished.

"Well, yes," said Christina. "It's the way you're dressed and all."

"Well, we've just been to a memorial service for my grandfather," answered Nicole.

"Do you mind me asking how you got here so fast?" Christina said.

"I was about to ask you the same question," said Nicole smiling. "My dad has to travel a lot on business, so he flies himself around.

"We had to make an emergency landing in Cleveland because of the storm. We actually live in Toledo, about 100 miles east of here," she added.

"Now, hold on one minute!" interjected Grant. "You *know* each other? How did that happen? Where was I? I WAS at the restaurant with you, Christina! How come..."

"Calm down, Grant," Christina pleaded. "They were there, and then they weren't. And now, here they are again!"

"So, are you on vacation?" asked Nicole.

"You could say that," Grant answered. "Mimi, our grandmother, is a mystery writer. We go on trips with her and our grandfather, Papa."

"Papa loves to fly us around in his airplane," Christina added.

"Yeah, the thing is, while Mimi does her on-site research, we sometimes end up deep in the middle of our own mystery to solve," Grant said.

Christina jabbed him in the ribs with her elbow.

"Ouch! What did I say?" yelped Grant.

"That's not always true, Grant." Her thoughts about the mysterious text message were making Christina nervous enough. Now Grant was reminding her that there very well could be another mystery brewing!

They walked over to the front desk, where Papa and Mimi were just finishing up a conversation with none other than Nicole and Dominic's dad!

"You must be Christina and Grant," he said. "Your grandparents were just telling me about your very interesting adventures! Well, welcome to our neck of the woods!"

"Thank you," Christina and Grant said in unison.

To Nicole and Dominic, their dad said, "These very nice folks have invited you on an adventure around the Great Lakes. It'll be a whole lot more interesting than sitting around on a boat watching me work. I'll always be close by. How does that sound?"

Grant and Dominic cheered and slapped a high-five. They raced to the window and peered out at the water. Christina and Nicole smiled, shrugged, and raced after them.

"Papa was just telling us about all the mysterious shipwrecks that happen in the Great Lakes," Grant breathlessly shared with their new friends.

"My dad dives for lost treasure for a living!" Dominic announced.

"We don't get to keep any of it, though," Nicole quickly added. "Insurance companies hire him to see if a wreck can be brought to the surface, or if its cargo can be salvaged."

"Why would cargo be savage? Were there a bunch of wild beasts on board when the ship went down?" Grant asked innocently.

"No, silly. Salvaged. It means saved," explained Christina.

"Well," said Dominic, pointing to the wreck out in the middle of Lake Erie, "when I saw that thing from the air, I thought it was some kind of beast—you know like the Loch Ness monster or something." His eyes sparkled with excitement.

"Oh, Dominic, there's no such thing as lake monsters," said his sister.

"Oh, there just might be," a voice said.

The kids whirled around and came face to face with a man wearing a hotel uniform. It was not the same one who checked them into the hotel.

"There's a local legend about a monster named Bessie," he said. "Mariners have been seeing our Bessie for centuries, up and down Lake Erie."

Christina felt goose bumps rise on her arms and legs. She leaned over and whispered to Grant, "The text message!"

Christina's mind raced with questions. *Is there really a lake monster? And who sent the message? How did they know we'd go to Lake Erie?* Things were getting scarier by the minute, and they had barely gotten started on their trip.

"Christina, are you okay?" Nicole asked.

"Well," Christina started and glanced over at Grant. Grant nodded. Christina was glad to have a brother who knew what she was thinking when it mattered most. "Remember when Grant hinted that mysteries seem to follow us on these trips we take?"

"Uh huh," Nicole said.

"Well, I think another one has just started!" Christina exclaimed.

CRACK! Another bolt of lightning lit the sky, this one much closer than the last.

"Let's get some sleep," Mimi said. You'll see your new friends at breakfast in the morning!"

"And by then the storm will have passed," Papa added.

As the kids said goodnight to each other, Christina glanced over her shoulder. What she saw made her knees go weak. Standing in front of the fireplace was the hotel desk clerk. Something was odd about the way his smile turned crooked as he peered into the fire. It wasn't the smile of a happy man. It was, she figured, something altogether different. Christina held on tighter to Mimi as they made their way to their hotel suite.

4
SHIPWRECK
SS GRANT

BOOM! The sound of thunder echoed in the hotel room. Christina opened one eye just enough to see the bright red glow of the digital clock by her bed. It was 8:15, the time school started back home. "Will these thunderstorms ever end?" she grumbled to herself. Christina yanked the covers over her head, trying to get back to sleep.

Grant bounded onto Christina's bed. "Are you awake?" Grant asked.

A muffled "No" came from under the covers.

"Mimi, Christina's not-awake self told me she's not awake!" Grant cried.

Mimi laughed and tugged on the covers at Christina's feet. "Excuse me, Christina's not-awake self, but it's time to get up."

"It's time to go see Elvis! Uh, huh!" Papa exclaimed.

Grant giggled. "You're silly, Papa. Elvis is dead."

"Right you are, Grant," Papa said, "but his music is still alive!" He began singing, "You ain't nothin' but a hound dog...cryin' all the time..." Grant joined in, strumming his air guitar.

Somehow between the storm, the lake monster, and the shipwreck story, Christina had almost forgotten all about where they were going today—the Rock and Roll Hall of Fame!

Christina tossed the covers aside and popped up like a jack-in-the-box.

"There's my girl!" Mimi shouted. "Good morning, sleepy head."

Christina slid out of bed. "Please," she said, "make them stop singing, Mimi. It's too early for that!"

Papa and Grant grinned and winked. "It helped get her up, right, pardner?" Papa said and pointed at the table. "Now, hurry up and eat your breakfast. To save time, we're eating breakfast in the room. We'll meet your friends downstairs."

Grant, Mimi, and Papa were already dressed and ready to go. Pellets of rain slammed against the hotel window, creating a drumming sound.

Christina raced around the hotel room getting ready. "Why didn't anyone wake me up earlier?" she asked, but managed to get dressed and eat in record time—jeans, BITE WAFFLE, sweater, CHEW, brush hair, SIP ORANGE JUICE, put on shoes, GULP!

"I'll pull the SUV underneath the awning, so we can load up without getting soaked," Papa suggested. "Grant, you come with me to help with the luggage. Christina, you stay with Mimi while she checks out downstairs."

Nicole and Dominic were saying goodbye to their dad when Christina got to the lobby.

"...so as long as we're within a 35-mile range of each other, you'll be able to reach me," Christina heard their dad say.

ee you later, Dad!" The kids said and
Christina and Mimi.

Once the SUV was loaded up, Papa
pulled onto the road, and headed for the Rock
and Roll Hall of Fame. Even though the
weather was quite nasty, with buckets of rain
and ground-shaking thunder, Christina didn't
let it get her mood down. Ever since Mimi had
told her about the trip, she couldn't wait to go
to the Rock and Roll Hall of Fame. And what
made it even better was sharing her
adventures with new friends!

Grant peered out the window. "You
didn't tell us there's a pyramid here," he said.

As they approached, Christina could
see two triangular buildings made almost
entirely of glass. Behind them were other
modular shapes.

"Whoa, that's so cool!" Christina
exclaimed.

"The Egyptians may have their own
pyramids, but these are even more awesome!"
Grant announced, his neck straining to see the
top of the building from the confines of the SUV.

Papa had terrific luck finding a parking spot close to the museum entrance. "Must be my lucky day!" he said.

"Ready for some rock and roll?" Mimi asked, looking back at the kids.

"Yeah!" Christina said.

Grant grinned. "Uh, huh! I'm all shook up," Grant sang, cocking his eyebrows to imitate Elvis.

The kids laughed.

Papa and the kids ran to the entrance. Mimi followed under a round red umbrella that reminded Christina of an apple. Once at the door, they could already see bright lights, some yellow, red, and green.

"It looks like a giant iceberg," Christina said.

"Yeah, especially because the water is right there!" Grant said.

Christina looked around. The building was surrounded by water!

Christina and Grant wandered to the side of the building, while Papa waited for Mimi to shake the water off her umbrella.

SLAP! Lake Erie lapped at the sea wall, splashing up and nearly soaking Christina and Grant. Grant leaned over to get a better look.

"Don't go too close, Grant," Nicole warned. "It's built right over the water—the whole thing!" she added.

Christina, wide-eyed, looked at Nicole and then tiptoed closer to the edge of the sea wall. She looked down at the dark, icy waters of Lake Erie. When she looked up, she could see the back of the museum and into the triangular glass buildings.

"Is that a car?" Christina asked.

"Where?" Grant said. He stared intently at the lake.

"No, Grant, inside the Hall of Fame," Christina said, "hanging from the ceiling!"

Grant quickly spun around, and the heel of his shoe caught a section of uneven pavement, sending him tumbling backward.

"OOOHHH!" Grant yelled as he slid onto the edge of the concrete sea wall.

Christina quickly turned to see her brother falling toward the rumbling lake water.

"Grant!" she shouted.

Though Grant's bottom was firmly planted on the top of the wall, his arm and entire right side dangled precariously over the side. If he moved, he'd fall and be a goner!

"Christina, help!" Grant yelled.

Christina raced to the wall and planted her foot at the base of it. She reached her hand out to Grant. "Grab my hand!" she shouted.

"I...I..." Grant yelled. He struggled to reach his sister's hand. His fingertips just touched hers, but they couldn't connect. "I CAN'T!" Grant wailed.

"Here," Nicole offered Christina. "Take my hand. Now reach for Grant." Christina took a deep breath and leaned over further. In one swift motion, she grabbed his arm and yanked her body backward, pulling Grant off the wall.

THUMP! All three tumbled to the hard walkway.

"Grant, Christina, Nicole, Dominic!" Papa yelled. "Where are you?"

"We're over here," Dominic called.

They scrambled to their feet and met Papa coming around the corner.

"Let's get this show on the road!" Papa said.

The kids followed Papa obediently into the museum, still breathing hard.

"Never do that again, Grant!" Christina whispered.

"Never again!" Grant promised.

This trip is getting wilder and wilder, thought Christina.

5
DANGLING CARS AND GUITARS

The first thing Christina did when she entered the building was look up. She just had to see those cars on the ceiling!

"Look!" Christina said, and pointed up at the three full-sized cars that hung from the rafters.

BA-BOOM...BA-BOOM...! A thundering guitar riff with a heavy beat filled the entry area. The sounds echoed due to the building's unusual shape.

"Cool!" Grant said. "I like the white car with words on it."

"I like the tiger-striped one," Christina remarked.

"The red spiked one's for me!" Mimi added.

Papa tilted back his cowboy hat. "I like them all, but I really want to go see some guitars."

Grant started to play air guitar again, drawing amused looks from other museum visitors. "Looks like a natural," said an elderly lady with two little girls in tow.

"Oh, he's a natural, all right," Papa replied. "A natural goofball!"

Grant giggled. "Papa, that's the nicest thing you've said to me all day!"

"Come on, Grant." Christina tugged at his arm. "I want to see some REAL guitars— not your hot air ones!"

"Wowwwwww," Christina mumbled as they passed through glass doors into the heart of the museum. Long hallways led to each exhibit, which were carefully labeled.

"Look!" Grant shouted. He pointed to a long white jacket in a glass case. "That's a Sergeant Pepper's Band jacket! It was worn by John Lennon!"

"One of the Beatles!" Dominic said.

Dominic sang, "Well, it was 20 years ago today, Sergeant Pepper taught a band to play."

Nicole joined in, "They've been going in and out of style, but they're guaranteed to raise a smile."

Christina picked it up from there, "So, may I introduce to you, the act you've known for all these years!"

Grant danced and pretended he held a microphone. "Sergeant Pepper's Lonely Hearts Club Band!"

Papa and Mimi laughed.

"Let's move on to the guitars!" Grant suggested, skipping down the hall.

They wandered down a hallway filled entirely with guitars. Every make, model, and color from different guitarists appeared to be there.

DING! Mimi's cell phone beeped. "Who could that be?" she asked. She pulled the red phone from her bag. "What?" Mimi looked confused at the text message.

"What's that all about?" Papa asked.

Mimi answered, "Well, Ichabod says he thinks the lighthouse is haunted. He's been hearing some strange noises and such. Lights going on and off."

The kids stopped in their tracks.

"Ghost?" Grant said. His eyes widened with interest.

"Well, I wouldn't be too worried, Grant," Mimi said. "Ichabod is old, and I'm thinking that he may be getting confused."

"Well, Papa said, "we still have a bit more of the museum to see, so let's get to it."

Christina leaned over and whispered to her brother, being careful not to let their friends hear. "I'm starting to think going to Mr. Ichabod's lighthouse is not a good idea at all."

"Me too," Grant said. "Between the ghost and Mr. Icky, I'm thinking we should skip that part of the trip."

"We can't, though," Christina said. "He's Mimi's friend, and she's worried about him."

"Right," Grant said.

BOOM! CRACK! Lightning and thunder jolted the kids back to reality. Christina shivered. *Now was there a ghost added to the mysterious mix?*

6

SLIPPERY SANDS

DING! DING! Christina's cell phone startled her. She was in the back seat of Papa's SUV with Grant and their new friends. They were on their way to the Great Sleeping Bear Dunes on Lake Michigan.

Mimi had called Mr. Wallace to update him on their whereabouts. Nicole thought that maybe her dad was calling back, but realized it was the wrong phone ringing.

"WAIT!" Grant whispered. "What if it's the monster?"

Christina paused, and considered what Grant had just said. "We'll look at it together," she suggested.

The kids nodded.

Christina slowly opened her phone. All four of them hovered over the phone as if she were unwrapping a birthday gift.

The text message read,

> I SEE YOU, BUT YOU CAN'T SEE ME. ROUND AND ROUND TO THE TOP. YOU'RE ALWAYS SCHEMING.

"What is THAT supposed to mean?" Grant asked.

Christina's hand shook as she held the phone. "It's a riddle, I guess." She read it again, but slower. "I see you, but you can't see me."

The kids looked around nervously. Papa was focused on the road, and Mimi was taking notes.

"Can't be from Mimi or Papa," Grant whispered.

"Yeah," Christina agreed and shook her head. "I was actually hoping that Mimi sent it. But she couldn't have."

Grant and Dominic popped their head up and looked back to see if anyone might be following them. There were no other cars on the road as far as they could see.

"So, what is something that can see us, but we can't see it?" Christina asked.

Grant gulped. "A ghost?"

Christina snapped the phone closed. "I don't know, Grant...maybe."

"But can ghosts send text messages?" Grant asked. Christina had already turned towards Nicole.

"So, this is what you meant when you said mysteries seem to follow you around!" Nicole said.

Just then Papa announced, "We're here!"

Papa's booming voice startled Christina, and she let out a tiny scream.

When they arrived at Great Sleeping Bear Dunes, the rain had stopped, but the sky was filled with clouds.

"Wow, that's a lot of sand," Grant commented.

"My dad said that the Great Sleeping Bear Dunes were formed during the Ice Age," Nicole explained. "And believe it or not, Lake Michigan was once filled with ice. When the glaciers moved through here, they crushed the rocks into sand. The wind piled the sand into great dunes, including the one shaped like a bear."

"That's how this national lakeshore got its name," added Dominic.

"Your friends are right," Mimi said. The kids all lined up in front of what looked like a giant wall of sand.

"Does the sand ever end?" Grant asked.

"It does," Papa said, "but you'll have to work to get there!"

"Sure glad I wore my sneakers today," Mimi said, looking down at her white shoes with red shoelaces. "We have a long climb ahead, kids," she reported.

"I'm so glad Dad agreed to let us climb the dunes!" Nicole said.

"Come on. Let's race!" Dominic dared Grant and the girls.

The kids ran past Mimi, ready to tackle the first dune. The air was crisp, and a cool breeze swirled sand into the air at the base of the dune.

At first they sprinted quickly, but as the dune got steeper, they found that the sand made their travel difficult. For every step they took, they slid backward a bit, the sand flooding downhill.

"Ugh!" Christina yelled.

"This is hard!" Grant said. "My shoes have a ton of sand in them!" The kids all flipped off their shoes, figuring carrying them would be easier than wearing them.

Christina stopped beside Nicole, whose hair had come loose from its hair band, leaving a tangled mess. Nicole reached up to smooth and retie her hair. Christina bent over with her hands on her knees and breathed hard. Grant and Dominic plopped down on the sand next to her.

"Whew. Need...to...catch...my breath," Christina managed to say between breaths.

"Me...too," Grant said.

Christina looked back. Mimi and Papa were way back, struggling just as they had. The kids had made it halfway across the dune before **collapsing**.

After a few moments of rest, they were ready to resume their climb.

"Okay, we're almost there," Grant said.

They made one last sprint to the top. But, when they crested the top of the dune, they felt their hearts sink. On the other side of the dune...were more dunes!

"NOOOO!" Grant and Dominic yelled.

"Come on, we made it this far," Christina said. The kids trudged together down the first dune and up the next small rise.

Surrounding the dunes were trees with magnificent autumn **foliage**. Bright reds, golden yellows, and brilliant orange-colored leaves danced in the breeze.

"Finally!" Christina said.

"We made it!" Dominic shouted.

The kids stood on top of the last rise. The steel-gray waters of Lake Michigan lapped at a small beach below them. They raced down the hill, thrilled to have finished their climb.

"WHOOOAAA!" Grant stumbled and tumbled, legs and arms flailing, down the dune, landing face first in the sticky, wet sand.

"PFFFTTT!" he sputtered. "I'm hungry, but a sand-wich was not what I had in mind at all!"

"Oohh, look!" Christina pointed out into the water. "There's something on the horizon. I think it's a boat!"

Grant scanned the waters. "Yup, I think you're right."

They watched the black dot on the horizon move closer and closer, and get bigger and bigger! "It's a tanker, Grant," Christina said. "It's a ship used by companies to transport stuff! They're huge!"

"So, big ships like tankers use these lakes?" Grant asked.

"Yes," Nicole said. "Big shipments of heavy cargo like iron ore or coal are often shipped on the Great Lakes. It's a lot cheaper than moving them on land by truck or by train."

"It's hard to imagine that the Great Lakes were once filled with fur trappers, traders, loggers, and then settlers who built cities like Chicago and Detroit," said Christina.

"Hmmmm," Grant said, splashing in the waters lapping at the shoreline.

Christina could tell her brother's interest in the impromptu social studies lesson was waning.

Papa and Mimi finally arrived, huffing and puffing. Papa carried a large bag.

"Surprise!" Mimi shouted, trying to catch her breath.

Papa plopped a bag onto a dry area of the beach. "We've brought along a picnic!" he said. "Then, we'll go out on the boat."

"Lunch? Great, I'm starved!" Grant yelled, motioning the others to follow. He ran over to help Mimi set up the food.

"Our boat?" Christina asked. "Out THERE?" She pointed to Lake Michigan sparkling in the few rays of sun still peeking through the clouds.

"Absolutely! It's the only way to get to the island," Papa said.

The thought of taking the little *Mimi* out on such a huge lake worried Christina. She was hoping for some great fall *fun*, but what she felt was serious fall *fear*. She didn't share these feelings with Nicole; she didn't get the sense that Nicole was even the slightest bit afraid.

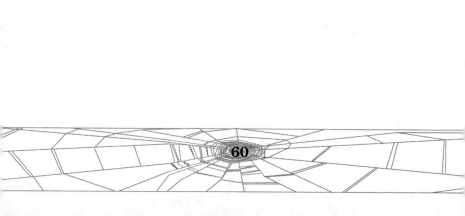

7
STRANDED ON NO-WHERE'S ISLAND

Papa stood in the little *Mimi* boat. "Okay, now, one by one. Ladies first," he said, holding out his hand for Mimi.

Christina was nervous, and really didn't want to go. "Papa, are you sure about this? I mean, is it safe?"

Papa nodded. "No problem, Christina. "People living in these parts go boating and fishing on the lakes all the time!"

"It's true, Christina," added Nicole, "there isn't anything to be worried about." When Mimi was safely aboard, Papa reached out his hand for Christina. Even though the air was cool, Christina felt sweaty.

She had managed to convince herself that something bad was going to happen, and it was hard for her to shake the feeling. Once Grant hopped on board, Papa started up the engine. BLUB, BLUB, ROAOARRR!

"Everyone seated with life vests on!" Papa shouted over the roar of the boat's engine.

"Aye, aye, Captain!" Grant shouted back to Papa.

Dominic needed a hand with the buckle on his life jacket, but then they were off. Christina buckled her life vest as tight as it would go. She clutched the edge of the little *Mimi* and watched as Papa **maneuvered** the boat out onto Lake Michigan.

The boat bounced and shook as it made its way over to the Manitou Islands. Wave after wave after wave crashed over the front of the boat.

"Wooo-hooo!" Grant shouted as the boat rose high, then crashed down into the water, spraying icy droplets onto the "crew."

Christina felt queasy from all the rocking and bouncing. She closed her eyes, trying to make the feeling go away.

"Christina, dear, don't close your eyes. It'll make it worse. Focus on the horizon," Mimi suggested.

"Land-ho!" Grant yelled.

An island seemed to rise up out of nowhere. It had tall, sandy cliffs. *Thank goodness,* Christina thought. She couldn't wait to get off this crazy boat ride!

Papa slowed the engines as they approached South Manitou Island. He pulled the *Mimi* close to the shoreline, into the small docking area.

Christina was the first to scramble off the boat. She was never so happy to be on land as she was then—even if being on land meant being in the middle of a monstrous lake!

She wriggled out of her life vest and gazed out onto the island. It looked barren, with nothing to be seen for miles!

"So, Mimi, is there anything here?" Christina asked.

"Sure there is," Mimi said. "Look."

Christina looked in the direction of Mimi's pointed finger. "A shipwreck? A real shipwreck?!" Christina yelled.

"Aye, lassies, let's go!" Grant said to Mimi and Christina, and tugged at Christina's sleeve.

Mimi smiled. "We'll get there, all in good time."

Papa fussed at the little *Mimi*. "Now, why aren't you cooperating?"

"What's wrong, Papa?" Christina asked.

"Well, seems like the little *Mimi* here doesn't want to be tied to the dock." He grunted and retied the knot. "Ah, there, that'll do it."

Papa climbed onto shore and looked at his watch. "Okay, we only have 20 minutes here, and then we'll need to head back."

"Why only 20 minutes, Papa? Grant asked. "We just got here!" He couldn't wait to stand on the deck of the stranded shipwreck, pretending he was a fearless pirate!

Papa wagged his finger at Grant. "Because the rules of the park state that is how long we can dock a boat. We need to follow the rules."

"So, let's get to that shipwreck, shall we?" Mimi said.

They hurried down the worn dirt path to the shipwreck. Suddenly, through a clearing in the trees, they could see what looked like a real ship sitting just off the coast. The kids picked up their pace.

When they moved through the clearing, the shipwreck came into complete view. It was massive! It looked like most of an entire ship was waiting for them out in the water.

The kids were lost for words. It was a scary sight, but also **intriguing**.

"How did a ship like that end up there?" Christina asked.

"That is the wreck of the *Francisco Morazan*," Mimi explained. "It met its fate in November 1960. A bad storm that rose out of nowhere caused the captain to turn back and seek shelter here in Manitou Islands. But the ship ran aground, and has been here ever since. Luckily, the crew and captain were all rescued."

"Wowwww!" the kids said together.

"But wasn't there a lighthouse?" Christina asked.

"What's a lighthouse got to do with a shipwreck?" Grant asked.

"A lighthouse guides ships," Papa said, "so that the crew can see the light in the dark, or sometimes during a storm. Some lighthouses even have horns for when the fog is thick as pea soup! But it's not foolproof. Sometimes the storms are so bad that even the brightest light from the lighthouse can't be seen," he added.

"Especially in the winter, when you have a whiteout," Nicole added.

"Whiteout? Is that like a blackout?" Grant asked. "When all the electricity goes out, and you can't play video games?"

"No. A whiteout is when there's so much snow falling and swirling in the air that you can't see anything but white," Mimi said.

Papa glanced at his watch. "We'd better head back."

Christina took one last look at the huge, hauntingly beautiful ship before heading back to their boat. "I wish it were summer, so we could take a swim and get a better look at the ship," said Christina.

"And this coming from someone who was afraid to come out here in the first place," taunted Nicole. "That's pretty brave. I don't think I would swim so close to a ship—even a shipwrecked one."

On the way back, Grant noted, "You know, I haven't seen any other people here at all."

Christina thought for a moment. "You're right, I haven't, either."

Mimi was the first to arrive back at the docks. "Is this the right dock?" she asked.

"Certainly. There's only one," Papa said.

Mimi shook her head. "Well, then, we're in deep trouble, because the little *Mimi* isn't here."

Mimi was right! The dock was empty and the boat was gone! The only thing left was the rope that Papa had tied to the little *Mimi,* and *that* was dangling in the water.

8
A CLOSE CALL

Papa scratched his head. "I don't know how she got free," he said. "I tied her down tight."

"I know, Papa. I watched you do it!" Christina cried. Christina had no intention of being stranded on an island in the middle of Lake Michigan. "We need to find the little *Mimi* boat," Christina exclaimed.

"Boats don't just disappear," Papa said.

"Unless they're shipwrecks," Grant added. "Oh, no! I hope the little *Mimi* wasn't swallowed by the lake, Papa!"

"Well, while storms do come up quick out here, I don't think that's what happened to our ship," Papa replied.

"Look!" Christina shouted. "There!" She pointed out a few yards into Lake Michigan. The little *Mimi* bobbed up and down with the waves.

Papa sat down and took off his shoes and socks.

"What are you going to do, Papa?" Grant asked.

"Get the little *Mimi*, of course," Papa said.

Papa rolled up his jeans to just above his knees. "I'm going to round up that stray pony," he said. He gingerly dipped his toes into the cold waters of Lake Michigan. "BRRRR! A bit chilly," he said.

DING! DING! Mimi pulled her cell phone from her pocket. "In the middle of nowhere, and I still get text messages," she said.

Grant and Christina watched while Mimi read the message. After only a few moments, her face grew pale and her eyes filled with concern. "Oh, dear. Oh, dear." She hurriedly tapped out her response.

"What's wrong, Mimi?" Christina asked, placing a hand on Mimi's shoulder.

"It seems Ichabod is so frightened that he won't spend the night any longer at the lighthouse." Mimi closed her phone. "It's not like him. Something is terribly wrong!"

Papa pulled the little *Mimi* back to shore by the rope that had broken off at the dock. It looked like he was leading a horse.

"What are you going to do, Mimi?" Christina asked.

Mimi answered, "Well, I told him to sit tight. We'll be there in just a few short days."

Mimi, Christina, Grant, and their friends walked toward the little *Mimi,* now fastened to the dock and waiting for their arrival. Everyone cheered. Papa rolled down his sopping jeans.

"Whoo-whee, that was cold water," he remarked. "Cold enough to wake the dead!"

Grant shot Christina a look. "All this talk about Mr. Icky being scared and shipwrecks and dead water is giving me the willies!" Grant said.

Christina nodded in agreement.

Mimi boarded the boat. "Not to worry, kids; there's no ghost. I'm certain that Mr. Ichabod is just not feeling well," she said. "Can you imagine that—Ichabod afraid of a few noises that go bump in the night?"

Christina wanted to go home, back to Georgia, and away from all this spooky stuff here on the Great Lakes.

But after the events with the little *Mimi*, a part of her was getting mad. *Did someone try to leave them high and dry on this isolated island?* She needed to find out!

9
PLAY IT "STRAIT"

Papa shook his fist at the gigantic freighter ship that passed the little *Mimi* boat so closely that it rocked her back and forth, tossing the kids out of their seats.

"Papa, stop yelling at them. They can't hear you anyway!" Mimi shouted over the roar of little *Mimi's* engine.

They were en route to their next destination. Papa had insisted on seeing the Straits of Mackinac, the waterway that connects both Upper Lake Michigan and Lake Huron, by boat. "Why should we drive over a long, boring bridge and only get a glimpse of the water?" he'd said.

And now Christina was certainly regretting his decision. But looking at their new friends smiling and excited about the next adventure made Christina feel just a tad guilty for wanting to end it right here and now.

They were heading through the strait to a lighthouse on Round Island on Lake Huron. Once around the hook of Mackinac Island, Papa turned the boat north.

"This is a very important stretch of water," Papa said.

Grant looked around. It didn't look any different from any other body of water he'd seen.

"Why's that Papa?" Christina asked.

"Wanna take this one, Dominic?" Papa asked.

Dominic answered, "Yes, sir. This is the only way to get between Lake Michigan and Lake Huron."

Then, Papa added, "That's right. Both lakes have many large cities that rely on the water to get their products back and forth. Lake Huron also touches Canada," Papa said.

"So that means you can also transport goods across Lake Huron and into Canada?" Christina asked.

"Sure does, Christina," Papa said. "Now, while Lake Michigan is the only one of the Great Lakes that lies entirely in the United States, the other Great Lakes all border both the United States and Canada."

"Wow, so that means we're near Canada?" Grant asked.

"Yep!" Mimi said. "And if it weren't for these Great Lakes and the ability to use the water for shipping goods, it would take a lot longer to move things around."

"But it's not always smooth sailing for the freighters," Papa said. "Can you tell us why that is, Nicole?"

"Yes sir. Sometimes the icy conditions make the lake impassible. The freighters have to wait for the cutters to actually clear lanes in the water so ships can pass. Or," Nicole added with enthusiasm, "the weather conditions are so horrible, they have to wait to set sail."

"And there is some pollution in the waters, mostly ore from wrecks," Mimi said with a frown. "And while sea creatures called zebra mussels help with pollution, they create a **nuisance** in another way."

"How's that, Mimi? How can it help, but hurt?" Christina asked.

"Ah," Mimi said. "The mussels attach themselves to everything underwater, including other shellfish."

"Wow, I didn't realize all that stuff was going on under the water!" Grant said.

Up ahead, Christina saw a tiny island with a tall red lighthouse and a modest red-and-white building beside it. The island was rocky with only a handful of trees.

"Is that IT?" Christina asked.

"Yep, that's where we're headed, to the Round Island Lighthouse," Mimi replied.

Christina wasn't very impressed. It looked old, and most of all, barren.

"Looks spooky, if you ask me," Grant commented.

Papa once again docked the boat and helped everyone off.

"Are we the only ones on the island? Again?" asked Christina.

"I reckon so," Papa said.

"Great," Christina muttered.

"No, Great LAKES!" Grant shouted.

Christina rolled her eyes at her brother's comment.

Mimi walked the island making notes, while Papa moored the boat. This time, he made certain she wasn't going anywhere. The currents were strong, but he tied her to several pylons.

"Let's go see the lighthouse," Grant suggested to Dominic.

Hearing his suggestion, Christina said, "I don't know..." But Grant and Dominic had already run off.

"Come on, Nicole," Christina said. "If I let him out of my sight, he's bound to get into trouble. He is good at that."

"Don't you remember, Christina? I've seen him in action! Let's go!" Nicole urged.

"Grant! Wait!" Christina shouted.

When the girls caught up to the boys, they'd already opened a creaky old door and stepped inside. The girls followed, closing the door behind them.

"Oooh, it's dark inside here," Christina commented. She spied a winding staircase leading to the light at the top. They caught up with the boys.

"Up we go!" Grant shouted. The kids climbed the steps as they wrapped around the lighthouse interior.

"Round and round she goes," Christina said.

"Up and around," Grant commented, and then stopped abruptly.

Christina, following just one stair behind her brother, bumped into him. "Hey, why'd you stop?"

"What did that last text message say again?" Grant asked.

Nicole peeked around Christina and said, "Something about round and round to the top?"

Christina yanked her phone out of her back pocket. She flipped it open and pulled up the message again.

Grant read the illuminated words aloud, "I see you, but you can't see me. Round and round to the top. You're always scheming."

"Maybe this means going around and around in the steps of a lighthouse?" Christina asked.

"Okay, but then what about the other part? 'I see you, but you can't see me?'" Dominic asked.

"I'm not sure yet," said Christina. She closed the phone and put it back in her pocket.

"Maybe we should tell Mimi and Papa about the message," Grant suggested.

"No, there's no need to. It's just a riddle. We're good at solving riddles," Christina said confidently.

"Okay," Grant said.

Nicole and her brother exchanged glances and shrugged.

"Go on," Christina said, and nudged him forward.

"Stop pushing!" Grant complained. "I'm going, I'm going!"

They trudged up the stairs. Christina peered over the edge of the glass-enclosed room. She could see Mimi and Papa walking around the island, and lots of colorful boats in the water. There were tankers, and boats with multi-levels, and even small boats like the little *Mimi*.

"I can't help but think that as far as lighthouses go, this one isn't all that special," Christina said, more to herself than to anyone in particular.

Nicole added, "But there are lots of boats out there, and this is a much smaller area for them to pass through."

"That's true," agreed Christina. "That makes this lighthouse pretty important."

"Oh, there's another one!" Grant shouted, pointing to another lighthouse across the Straits of Mackinac.

Christina closed her eyes and imagined being on a ship at night and having to use the lighthouse's signal to guide her way.

GRRAWWWRRR! A loud noise startled the kids. They all jumped, and Grant moved closer to Christina.

"Wha, what was that?" Grant stuttered.

"I don't know!" Christina screeched. "But it came from down there!" She pointed to the bottom of the lighthouse.

"Now what?" Dominic implored.

Christina looked around and realized that they were trapped. The only exit was back down the stairs, where the sound came from!

"Kids? You in here?" Papa's big booming voice echoed up the steps of the lighthouse.

The kids let out a collective sigh at the sound of Papa's voice.

"Papa!" Grant shouted.

"Yes, Papa, we're up here!" Christina said.

"Well you best come back down. You're not supposed to be in here, you know?" Papa said gently, but firmly.

"Okay, we're on our way. Sorry, Papa," Christina said.

All four kids bounded down the steps one after the other. Papa stood just outside the old door.

Once outside, Papa closed the door. "Didn't you read the sign?" Papa asked.

"What sign?" Christina asked.

"This one." Papa pointed to a faded sign on the door. It read KEEP OUT.

"My fault, Papa. I guess I was too excited to explore the lighthouse," Grant confessed.

Papa said, "Okay, well, we need to be off. Seems the weather is kicking up, which is making quite a stir on the lake."

A gust of wind blew, swirling Christina's brown hair around her face.

Mimi was already aboard the boat when Papa returned with the kids.

"Oh, hurry, children. There's a storm approaching, and we need to get to Mackinac Point quickly!" Mimi said. "And put on those life jackets!" She held her bright yellow hat onto her head as another wind gust almost took it away.

Papa pushed the boat away from the dock, and they were back out in the Mackinac Straits.

The little *Mimi* was tossed back and forth, as the growing waves battered her hull.

"Hold on, everyone!" Papa yelled. "Big waves coming right at us!"

Mimi held onto her hat and shouted to the kids, "Now we know firsthand just how quickly these storms can come up out here."

Christina looked over at Grant, who looked a pale shade of green. As the boat hit a particularly huge wave, Grant doubled over. BLAAAAHHH! He threw up over the side of the boat.

Mimi leaned over to help him. "At least you have good aim, Grant," she said, winking at Christina.

Fortunately, they were near the shore. Papa docked the boat as quickly as he could on Mackinac Island.

Christina was ready for dry land—and a dry bed. She knew she would sleep well tonight. She would forget about text messages and storms and lighthouses and ghosts and everything else for a while!

10

CHEEKS AND PITS FOR DINNER

Christina quickly forgot her concerns once she set foot on Mackinac Island. Elegant Victorian buildings with flowerboxes overflowing with vibrant blooms lined the main street. Tall, muscular horses pulled carriages filled with waving tourists, not the least bit upset by the stormy skies. Bicycles whizzed by, weaving their way around the buggies.

"It's like we just stepped back in time!" Christina exclaimed. "Why aren't there any cars anywhere?"

"Because they're not allowed here," Dominic explained. "Tourists and residents get around by walking, riding bikes, or traveling in horse-drawn carriages. Pretty cool, huh?"

Grant nodded. "But what does that say?" he asked, pointing to a sign in curly Victorian script. "Is that how you spell the island's name? It's spelled M-a-c-k-i-n-a-c, but you have been saying Mackinaw!"

"Well," Nicole began, "we learned on a field trip that the pronunciation is 'Mackinaw' because it was named by an aboriginal tribe way back in prehistoric times. The tribesmen stood on the mainland and looked over at this island and saw large, high cliffs. To them, it looked like a giant reptile, and they called it mish-la-mackin-naw."

"Misha-mash-what?" Grant asked.

"Well," Nicole continued, "mish-la-mack-in-naw, in their language, meant large turtle. And seeing that this island would be very green in the summer, and round..."

"That it would look like a turtle to someone!" Christina added.

"So, we pronounce it as they would have," Nicole said, "with an 'aw' at the end, instead of the 'ac' that we see at the end."

"I get it," Grant said.

"I hope you're hungry," Mimi said as she turned to face the kids, 'cause we're here." She led them into a quaint restaurant humming with life and full of unfamiliar food smells. Condensation covered the windows, making seeing outside an impossibility.

Mimi had ordered something very special for them to eat. The waiter brought four bowls filled to the brim with a steamy, creamy soup.

"Hope you enjoy your walleye cheek chowder," he stated.

"Wall what?" Christina asked.

Grant took his spoon and pushed the soup around. He expected to see giant paint flecks and googly eyeballs. He sniffed the bowl. "Smells like fish," he said, looking rather uncertain about the whole thing.

"It's a fish called a walleye that is plentiful here in the Great Lakes. It's good, try some," Mimi added.

Christina spied her friends eating the soup with gusto. She dipped her spoon tentatively into the soup, so as not to get too much at first. She took a slurp. It reminded her of clam chowder, but had a slightly different taste.

"Umm," Christina said, and filled her spoon again.

Grant watched Christina eat first. He figured if she liked it, he'd give it a try, even if it might have eyeballs in it.

Christina took a bite and jumped! CLANK! Grant dropped his spoon and pushed the bowl away.

"That does it! I'm not eatin' that!" Grant announced.

"No, it's not the soup, silly," Christina said. "It's my phone. I had it on vibrate and just got a message."

Grant scooted closer to her. While Christina opened the phone underneath the table, Grant leaned down so they could talk in private. Nicole and Dominic were avidly discussing culinary delights with Mimi and Papa.

The text message read,

> YOU SAW THE SIGN, BUT WENT IN ANYWAY. JUST LIKE THERE, YOU'LL HEAR MY BOOTS ON THE STAIRS.

"Christina, we went into the lighthouse even though I saw the 'keep out' sign," Grant reminded her.

Christina nodded. "And we heard a loud noise, like something was on the steps," she said with a gulp.

"Do you think the person sending this," Christina asked, swallowing hard, "could be a ghost?"

"Yes, I do," Grant whispered, his blue eyes serious.

"Well, with that riddle solved, we now have an even bigger mystery on our hands," Christina said.

"And what's that?" Grant asked.

"Where this ghost is, and why he..."

"Or she," Grant interrupted.

"Or she, is sending us text messages!" Christina finished.

She and Grant popped back up to the table before anyone noticed.

Nicole was not at the table. When questioned, Mimi told them that Nicole's dad had called her on Mimi's cell phone.

Hmm, Christina thought, *if Mr. Wallace had Mimi's cell phone number, then Mimi or Papa might have given him hers too. Could he have been following them around? Could he be the one who's been leaving text messages?* Christina kept that hunch to herself and smiled when Nicole returned.

"That was your dad?" Christina asked.

"Yes," Nicole replied. "He's in the area planning his next shipwreck dive. He said he'd be on Lake Superior tomorrow with his crew, so he'll be close by."

"That's great," Christina said. Then, she asked Mimi if she could be excused to use the bathroom.

Papa rubbed his stomach. "That was the best walleye cheek chowder I've ever had."

Nicole and Dominic agreed wholeheartedly, and Grant just nodded. He hadn't touched his soup since the text message arrived. Although his soup was probably cold by now, the mystery was just getting hot!

11
THE FITZGERALD PERIL

The kids piled into the back of Papa's big SUV. They had been driving for hours, heading over to the last of the Great Lakes on their tour, Lake Superior.

On the long ride, Grant and Christina shared the latest text message with Dominic and Nicole.

"A ghost? Really? What makes you think it's a ghost?" Nicole asked, with sincere curiosity.

"Who else could it be? No one knows my cell phone number except my friends back in Georgia, and well, Mimi and Papa. A ghost is all we've got," Christina said.

"But a *ghost*?" Nicole repeated.

"It *is* pretty farfetched, huh?" Christina conceded. Christina was less and less sure that it was Nicole's father. She couldn't imagine why he would try to scare four kids.

Grant squirmed in his seat. "Are we there yet?" he asked.

"Almost. And this is going to be the best part of the trip," Mimi said.

"Why?" asked Christina.

"Well, because here we'll get to learn about the most famous shipwreck of all, the *Edmund Fitzgerald*!" Mimi exclaimed.

Christina knew that Mimi's new mystery book was about the wreck of the *Edmund Fitzgerald*.

"Who is Edmund Frizzle?" Grant asked.

Christina laughed. "Edmund Fitzgerald. It was the name of a ship."

"Right. So, why is this boat named after a guy?" Grant asked.

"Ships have names, just like people," Papa explained. "They sometimes are named for the person who built them, or designed them. Or sometimes, it's to honor a king or queen."

"That's interesting, 'cause until now, I always thought ships were only named after ladies," Grant said.

"Ships are referred to as 'she' no matter what their name is," Mimi explained.

"So, why is that wreck so famous?" Christina asked Mimi.

Mimi turned around to face the kids. "Well, there are a couple of reasons," she said. "The 'Mighty Fitz,' as she was nicknamed, was the largest ship on the Great Lakes when she was launched in 1958. Then, in November 1975, she sank. A wicked winter storm had been pounding her for a while, and she was headed for safety when she sank suddenly on Lake Superior. No distress signal, nothing. The entire crew of 29 died in the wreck. But I think what added to the attention of the disaster was that a song was written about the ship."

"That's right!" Papa shouted. "A fellow by the name of Gordon Lightfoot wrote it."

Papa thought for a few moments then belted out the tune. "The legend lives on from the Chippewa on down, of the big lake they call GitCHEEEE GuMEEEE." Papa continued to sing while he drove on.

"Gitche who me?" Grant asked.

Nicole laughed. "Gitche Gumee. It's an American Indian name, from the Algonquian language, for the lake. An American Indian tribe called the Chippewa lived here long ago, and they named the lake."

"I didn't know the Chippewa Indians were here," Christina said.

"It's true," Nicole continued. "And to this day, you'll see a lot of their influence still here, mainly in the names of places."

Though the tune Papa was singing was sad, it was interesting. Christina wanted to hear more. "Papa, can you sing it again?" she asked.

"Sure can," Papa said and gave his rendition of the folk song. The lyrics were of a November turned gloomy and a lake that never gives up its dead. Christina sat back in her seat and imagined what it must have been like for the sailors who risked everything sailing the Great Lakes for a living.

Papa pulled into the parking lot of the Great Lakes Shipwreck Museum. The museum included several small, crisply painted white houses against the sparkling blue waters of Lake Superior.

"You know, it's really beautiful here," Christina commented.

"The Great Lakes have some of the most incredible scenery in the country," Mimi agreed, throwing her arm around Christina's shoulder. "And you know how I love the water!"

"Wow," Christina commented. She pointed to a sign by a hefty brass bell. "It says that this bell was recovered from the *Edmund Fitzgerald* itself. It weighs 200 pounds! That's more than Grant and me put together!"

Grant scratched his head. "It doesn't make sense to me, Papa."

"What doesn't, Grant?" Papa asked.

"Well, the story here," he said, pointing to a plaque with a picture of the *Edmund Fitzgerald*. "It says here that the captain was in communication with the Coast

Guard, and he said they were holding their own. Then, all of a sudden, they lost the signal, and she sank."

Christina and Nicole joined Grant, Dominic, and Papa at the information site.

"Well, Grant, that's part of the mystery and tragedy of this ship," Papa said, as he turned his attention to the maps on the wall.

"Yeah," piped in Dominic, "they believe that it was a rogue wave, a very giant and dangerous wall of water, that sank the *Fitzgerald*."

"And they say it broke in half like the *Titanic* did," added Nicole. Papa turned his attention to the children again. Christina asked, "Papa, it also says here that the *Edmund Fitzgerald* and another ship, the *Anderson*, had no guidance from the lighthouse because it lost its radar. And it was in a blinding snowstorm. So how could they see where they were going?"

"Well, they used radio communications to talk with each other and the Coast Guard," Papa said. "That's how they also knew that there had been rogue waves. The other ship, the *Anderson*, had reported seeing them."

"So, it snows up here in November?" Grant asked.

Mimi laughed. "It does more than that," she said. "Ice builds up on the Great Lakes and ice breaker ships have to make lanes so the ships can pass."

"When the lakes freeze over, I bet you skate on them, right?" Grant asked Dominic.

"I wish, but it would be too dangerous. The ice is shifting. It's like icebergs; they float on top of the water," Dominic added.

"This is really sad," Nicole said, reading a sign. "Listen to this. When they had the memorial service at the Maritime Cathedral for all 29 members of the crew, they rang a bell 29 times, once each for the lost crew members."

"What is a marry time?" Grant asked.

"Maritime refers to boating and the water," Papa said. "For instance, we follow maritime law on the waters for safety and directions."

DING! Mimi's phone rang. She scanned the message quickly. "It's Ichabod. He's still not doing well, but he knows we're on our way. We should be there tomorrow."

"Mimi," Christina said. "Is it possible that Mr. Ichabod's place is really haunted?"

"Well, it is a very old lighthouse," Mimi thought aloud, and tapped her finger on her lip. "He said he heard footsteps going up the stairs of the lighthouse at night. I'm thinking it was just his imagination getting away from him."

Christina looked at Grant.

"Well, I have all the information I need here, let's get a move on," Mimi said and walked toward the door.

"Mr. Icky heard footsteps coming up his lighthouse," Grant said.

"You don't suppose..." Christina wondered aloud.

12
HOME OF THE DEVIL

DING! DING! Another message arrived on Christina's cell phone. Grant leaned in.

It read,

> BEWARE OF THE DEVIL'S MOUTH.
> IT CAN SWALLOW YOU WHOLE!

"Devil's mouth?" Grant asked.
"Hmmm, I wonder," Christina said.
"Wonder what?" The other kids asked impatiently.
"You know where we're going next, don't you?" Christina asked.

Grant thought for a minute. "No, where?"

"Devil's Island!" Christina announced.

Nicole and Dominic withdrew some kind of electronic device from Nicole's backpack and fiddled with the controls.

Grant leaned in close to Christina and asked, "What I want to know is how whoever is sending the text messages always knows where we're going!"

Christina looked at their friends and then back at Grant. The look on Grant's face was of utter shock, then disbelief.

"You don't think...that's impossible!" But then Grant watched them closely. They had what looked like a walkie talkie. They were trying to get it to work.

"When did you get that?" Grant asked Dominic.

"Our dad gave it to us before we left the hotel," he answered.

"I don't even think it works," Nicole said.

"I'll bet it's the batteries," said Grant.

Nicole rearranged the batteries. They heard static. "It works!" Nicole said. "It's supposed to reach a distance of 35 miles. My dad has the other one," she added.

"It's not them, Christina," whispered Grant.

Christina nodded and looked up to see a tall, white lighthouse. "Then, I'll bet we'll find our answers up there." She pointed to the lighthouse.

Papa docked the little *Mimi* and they all headed for the kayak launch.

Papa and Mimi climbed into one kayak, while Grant and Christina settled into another. A third one was reserved for Nicole and Dominic.

They set off with Christina in the back and Grant in the front. "Wait, Grant!" Christina yelled as Grant paddled both oars wildly. Their kayak moved in one direction, then the other. Christina looked down and saw pedals, like those on a bicycle.

"Grant, stop paddling!" Christina shouted.

Nicole and Dominic were having no problems at all maneuvering the kayak, and this embarrassed Christina.

"There are pedals, Grant, and I think we're supposed to use those to move us forward," Christina said hopefully.

Both Grant and Christina started pedaling. It was like riding a bike, but with your legs out in front. Grant and Christina's kayak started moving forward. Grant tried to paddle with the oars too, and his feet slipped off the pedals.

"How do you do this?" Grant yelled loud enough for Dominic to hear.

"Use the pedals to go forward and the oars to steer," Dominic yelled.

Grant resumed pedaling and the kayak slid forward. Faster and faster they went.

"Woo-hoo!" Grant yelled.

Christina glanced over at her friends and smiled slyly. A pseudo race had ensued. Papa and Mimi were way behind them, struggling with the kayak pedal system, too.

As they approached Devil's Island, they could see the lighthouse on top of the rocky shore.

"Whoa, that's cool!" Grant called.

"Caves!" yelled Dominic.

"Wow! Let's go to the lighthouse first, though," Christina said.

The kids found a cozy harbor for their kayaks. They hopped out and raced up a winding path cut through the pine trees. The frigid air hurt Christina's throat as she breathed.

They could see the entrance up ahead. The lighthouse was thin and white, completely round except for some metal support structure on the outside. It looked like a beautiful ivory tower against the cloudless blue sky.

"Living in the area, you'd think we'd have visited this place before now," Nicole exclaimed.

Christina felt a little guilty about suspecting their friends' dad. Now, it seemed just downright absurd. "I'm glad your dad let you come!" The kids abruptly stopped at the entrance, bending and huffing and puffing from exertion. Christina placed her finger on her lips. "Shhh, let's try to be quiet so we can surprise them."

The other kids nodded.

CREEEEAAACCCKKK! The rickety metal door moaned as Christina slowly pushed it open. The others followed her into the lighthouse. The waters splashing into the caves below created a loud, booming sound.

They crept up the steps one by one. Each step they took brought them one step closer to solving the mystery—they hoped!

Christina looked up to see that the steps ended soon at the top of the lighthouse. She held her breath for a moment, steadying her nerves.

Christina carefully took the last few steps, and at the top, she hopped onto the landing.

"HA!" she yelled.

"Gotcha!" Grant shouted as he jumped next to Christina.

13
SWALLOWED BY THE DEVIL

Christina and Grant were shocked to find that they were all alone. There was no one there!

"But I thought..." Christina started.

"You thought we'd find our answer here. Guess you were wrong," Grant said.

"Well, then, WHO is sending us these messages? They know where we are and where we're going. It doesn't make any sense," said Christina.

"Well, one thing is for sure," Grant said, "whoever is sending these messages has got to be in a lighthouse. Which one, however, is still a mystery."

They turned around to find that they truly were alone! Nicole and Dominic were gone!

"But, they were right behind us!" Christina exclaimed.

"Now, I'm scared!" Grant could barely get the words out.

"You mean you weren't scared before?" Christina said.

"What do you think happened to them?" Grant asked, ignoring her question.

"There's only one way to find out," Christina said. "On the count of three, okay? One, two, three—GO!"

With Christina leading the way, they bounded down the steps and pushed through the lighthouse door.

"What happened? Was anyone there? Did they hurt you?" It was Dominic. He was leaning against an oversized rock near the entrance to the lighthouse. His sister was standing next to him with her arms crossed, a look of concern on her face.

"What? No! We're fine. We thought something happened to you!" Christina said, exasperated.

"To be honest, I got scared," Nicole said. "I'm not brave like you, Christina. Grant, I'm sorry."

"It's okay," Grant said. "It was just another dead end anyway."

Christina sat down and put her head in her hands. She looked up and sighed.

"Oh, Christina," Nicole said, "I really want to help you. I just chickened out this time. So," she continued, "if it's not this lighthouse, then which one is it? Any ideas?"

"There are hundreds here on the Great Lakes," Christina said, then added, "I have an idea. We don't have the right lighthouse, but that shouldn't stop us from exploring those caves."

The kids raced back to their kayaks and climbed in. They pushed off the shore with the paddles and started to pedal once the kayaks were free-floating in the water.

"Let's try that one!" Grant pointed to a small cave.

"Over here," yelled Nicole. "That one is too difficult. Let's try one with a bigger entrance."

They pedaled and paddled around the side of Devil's Island until they spotted a sizeable cave entrance.

"Let's try this one; it should be much easier to manage," Christina said, and everyone agreed.

"Oooh, it's cold in here," Christina commented and rubbed her arms.

"And it smells like mushrooms and dirt too," Grant added, wrinkling his nose. "Let's go in further," he said, launching them deeper into the cave.

"Go slower, Grant!" Christina warned.

Christina and Grant continued to go deeper and deeper into the cave. Christina turned to see Nicole and Dominic wavering at the entrance.

"Come on, Nicole. It's amazing," Christina yelled.

"We're coming!" Nicole answered. Nicole and Dominic rowed over to get a better look in the cave.

Christina marveled at the stalactites hanging from the ceiling.

"They look like teeth!" Grant shouted.

Then it clicked in Christina's head!

"Teeth! Grant, you solved it! Our phantom text messenger must have meant that the Devil's Mouth is the caves!"

"YESSSS!" Grant exclaimed. But his joyous expression suddenly changed. "Weren't we supposed to avoid the Devil's Mouth? Something about swallowing us whole, right?" he asked.

"Uh, yeah, something like that," Christina replied. "But I don't think we're in danger here. The water is calm."

"Okay. If you say so," Grant replied.

"Let's try that smaller cave now. I think we have the hang of this crazy kayak now," said Christina.

"But shouldn't we heed the advice of the text message?" warned Nicole.

"The messages are just to scare us. Come on. It'll be fun," said Grant.

They had just enough room to swing the kayak around and pedal back out to the waters beyond the cave.

They had to work against the natural currents, so it took a while. Christina looked back. Nicole and Dominic were having trouble maneuvering their kayak. Christina knew she couldn't go back for them. She and Grant were right there at the mouth of the cave. They had a straight shot in.

"Duck!" Grant yelled suddenly, realizing their heads were going to hit the mouth of the cave. He buried his head in his chest.

Christina did the same, but because she was taller than Grant, her head scraped the top.

"OUCH!" Christina yelled.

Christina's head hurt a lot. She reached up and felt the warm stickiness of fresh blood.

Grant turned around to check on Christina. But his movement unbalanced the kayak, threatening to tip it over.

"Grant sit down, and don't move!" Christina shouted.

Grant plopped back into the kayak seat.

"Are you okay?" Grant asked.

"Yeah, I'm fine," Christina lied. She didn't want to give Grant a reason to want to leave the cave.

Grant wasn't going to make the same mistake twice, so instead of turning around to see if their friends were behind them, he yelled, "Dominic, are you in the cave?" No answer. "Christina, can you see them?"

"No. They were having some trouble against the current last I saw," Christina replied.

This cave, though much smaller, allowed them access to other tinier caves. Christina and Grant paddled into as many as they could, fascinated by the formations inside each one.

"Time to get out of here. Mimi and Papa are probably looking for us," Grant said, then added, "We should head back the way we came in."

"Either I'm growing, or this ceiling is shrinking!" Christina remarked.

Grant looked around. "Wait a minute. Where's that creepy-looking rock that was sticking out right around here?"

"OH MY GOSH!" Christina shouted. She noticed varying levels of water marks on the walls of the caves that she hadn't seen before. "We're not growing or shrinking! The water is rising!"

"And we're about to be eaten by the Devil's Mouth!" Grant cried.

14

UP LAKE SUPERIOR WITHOUT A PADDLE

"We have to get out of here!" Christina yelled.

Grant pedaled frantically, and the kayak raced ahead, slamming into the mouth of the cave. Rushing waves shook and rocked the little kayak.

"Hurry, Christina! I don't want to be lunch for some cave-dwelling creature!" Grant cried.

Christina tried to maneuver the kayak, but the swift current yanked the paddle from her hand.

"NOOOOO!" Christina screamed as she watched the paddle float away into an adjoining cave. "Grant, I need your paddle!"

Okay!" he said. "But how am I going to get this to you?"

"I don't know..." Christina wrangled with the problem.

Grant panicked and tossed the paddle blindly over his head. SLAM! It fell between him and Christina, slapping the kayak and sliding off into the water.

The paddle drifted toward a cave entrance and disappeared in its recesses.

"Did you get it?" Grant yelled, terrified to move or even look back.

"No, it's gone." Christina felt like crying.

Christina braced her hand on the ceiling and started to push. She glanced over at the entrance. THUMP! Christina felt the top of her head whack the roof of the cave again. The sound of the rushing waters grew louder and echoed in the empty caves.

Holding her head, she yelled, "We need to get the heck out of here!"

"What?" Grant shouted.

"OUT!" Christina screamed.

She couldn't help but be a little mad at her new friends. Why hadn't they tried harder to follow them? Maybe they could have helped.

"We could wait it out," Grant asked tentatively. The waves were deafening as they crashed just outside the cave. "The water has to go down, right?"

"And get stuck in here overnight—without a flashlight? NO WAY!" Christina cried.

Christina scooted down low into the kayak. She grabbed the side of the cave and pulled, the rough stone digging into her palms.

"Hey, what's that?" she asked. "I can hear someone just outside the cave."

"Look!" Grant squealed. "A rope!"

Grant pedaled and pedaled, inching the kayak forward. Christina leaned out of the kayak. It wobbled and nearly overturned.

"Got it!" Christina yelled. "Grant, can you get out of the kayak?"

"I think I can!" Grant replied.

"You ready? Like Papa always says, 'on the count of three,' okay? One, two, three, jump!" Christina yelled and plunged in! The frigid water engulfed the children.

"Look, the kayak is stuck in the entrance. That might have been us!" Grant said.

"It's a good thing the rope didn't get tangled in it!" Christina said. "We'll have to swim under it. Hurry before the water rises even more!"

They unbuckled their life jackets and slipped them off. Holding onto the life jackets, they swam over to the kayak.

"You go first, okay?" Christina said through chattering teeth. "Just hold your breath and pull yourself along the rope. It's not that far to the outside. I'll be right behind you."

"See ya soon, sis," Grant said, letting go of his life jacket and disappearing beneath the surface. The kayak scraped against the cave entrance. Christina took one last look around. A small crack in the rock a hundred feet up allowed faint sunlight to filter in. A leafy plant had taken root.

Christina took a deep breath and went under. The cold was numbing. She popped up on the outside of the cave to applause and a very teary-eyed Mimi. A bright white motorboat bobbed up and down, its motor humming. Christina held onto the rope as someone pulled her alongside the boat.

"Grab my hand, Christina." It was Mr. Wallace, Nicole's dad. Grant stood next to him wrapped in a huge towel, along with Mimi, Papa, Dominic, and Nicole.

Mimi fussed with Christina, wrapping her in a towel and hugging her.

"Thank goodness you're okay," Mimi cried.

"You two gave us quite the scare," Papa chimed in.

"I'm sorry, Papa and Mimi." Then Christina turned to Grant. "You did great, brother!" And she gave him a hug. "But, Mr. Wallace, how did you know we were here?" asked Christina.

"When Nicole saw the danger you were in, she called me on the walkie talkie," Nicole's dad answered.

Christina turned to Nicole and hugged her. "Thank you, Nicole."

"I'm just glad you and Grant are okay," Nicole said. "We finally made it into the cave. We searched for you in a couple of the passageways, but we couldn't find you. That's when we noticed the water rising. When you didn't answer our calls, we had to do something," she added.

Christina smiled. *They hadn't left them after all*, she thought.

15
ICY GHOSTS

Christina and Grant knew that no amount of begging could make their friends stay. Their dad had finished his work. It was time for them to go home. They said their good-byes and promised to call.

Christina and Grant stood just outside the Little Sand Bay Visitor Center. Mimi and Papa were busy cleaning up after their picnic lunch at the lakeside.

"My phone! I hear my cell phone," Christina cried.

"It's in Mimi's purse," Grant reminded her. "Remember, you gave it to her to hold before we went kayaking."

Christina retrieved her phone from Mimi's bag and popped it open. She readied herself for the next clue. Grant drew in close.

This time the message read,

```
JUST ONE ISLAND AWAY, IS WHERE
I STAY, AND AWAIT FOR YOU TO BE
NOSY!
```

"I'm not NOSY!" Grant said. He folded his arms across his chest. "Hmmmh."

"You kinda are," Christina chided. She closed the phone.

"So are you!" Grant retorted.

"Okay, okay!" Christina admitted. "But, maybe being nosy will help us solve this mystery. We need a better map of the area."

Grant eyed the visitor's center. "Bet you they'll have a map!"

"True, and Mimi and Papa said we'd be going in there to get a bandage for my head," Christina said.

"Is your head okay?" Grant asked.

"Yeah. It's nothing but a scratch, but you know Mimi," Christina said.

Grant nodded. Mimi always wanted to make any "ouchies" feel better.

"Hello!" A woman with curly black hair and a wide smile greeted them at the door. Her nametag read 'Susan.' "Welcome to Little Sand Bay and the Apostle Islands," she said.

"Well, thank you kindly," Papa said. He pushed back his cowboy hat. "Do you happen to have some bandages, and maybe some first-aid cream?"

"Of course, right here." The woman handed Papa a personal-size first-aid kit that she kept behind the counter.

"Perfect!" Mimi said. "Christina, come over here, please."

As Christina approached, the saleswoman saw her cut. "Oh, dear! You've got quite the bump. I hope it doesn't hurt too bad."

"No ma'am," Christina said.

Mimi applied some first-aid cream, and then placed the bandage on Christina's scrape.

"There, good as new!" Mimi said.

"So, are you here for adventure?" the clerk asked.

"Yup!" Grant answered. "Shipwrecks, lighthouses, caves—all of it!"

"Ah, so you saw the caves! What did you think?" she asked.

"They were awesome! Well, except for Christina hurting her head, and us getting trapped in them," Grant replied.

"OH, MY!" the woman said. "These waters can be very treacherous. Storms come in so quickly sometimes, you barely have time to grab your coat and skedaddle."

"That's what we've heard. Especially when we went to visit the *Edmund Fitzgerald* museum," Mimi said.

"Do you have any shipwreck stories?" Grant asked.

The saleswoman grinned. "Oh, I do. You know, there are many, many tales, but let me tell you the scariest one. You like scary stories, right?" she asked.

Grant's blue eyes grew wide. He was so taken by the offer to hear a scary story that he was made speechless. He simply nodded his head.

"Sure, I'd like to hear a scary story," Christina said.

The woman began, rubbing her hands together. "Well, I told you how storms come up quickly around these parts, but even more so on Lake Superior than on any of the other Great Lakes. The size of the lake and its northernmost location add up to some pretty nasty weather conditions.

"Back in November of 1886," she continued, "there was a beautiful schooner ship on the lake." She paused for dramatic effect. "A schooner is a boat with two large sails, in case you didn't know that."

Grant nodded. *She seems really nice,* he thought.

"Anyway," the woman continued, "this one, the *Lucerne*, had huge new sails, and shiny new brass riggings. The ship was to sail to Cleveland along the Great Lakes. Even though there was fine weather to start, a nor'easter came rolling in."

"What's a north Easter?" Grant asked. He pictured the Easter bunny dressed in earmuffs and a down jacket.

Papa answered, "A nor'easter is a storm that always comes sweeping in from the north. It's usually very strong and cold with lots of snow."

Christina had goose bumps. She wasn't certain if it was because of all the talk about snow and ice, or if the story was creeping her out.

"Exactly," the woman said. "Well, the captain knew he couldn't make it to land, much less even find the land, since the storm was so ferocious. So, he dropped anchor instead, hoping to ride it out."

"They didn't, did they?" Grant guessed.

"No," she replied, "the ship sank and was discovered in the morning after the storm had cleared. When they finally made it out to the ship, several men were still lashed to the masts, their bodies frozen in a glistening coating of ice."

Christina gasped.

"That *is* scary," Grant agreed.

"Well, that just shows how powerful these storms can be, and how quickly they come up," Mimi said.

"Thanks for the tale. We appreciate it," Papa said. "I think?" he whispered, nudging Mimi.

Grant spotted a map. He tugged at Christina's sweater. "Over here."

Christina and Grant stepped to the map display, where Christina quickly selected a map of Lake Superior. Christina peered over the top of the map. Mimi and Papa were a safe distance from them. They were chatting with the store clerk.

"Okay, we're here," she said, pointing to a spot on the map.

"So, that means our clue tells us to go here," Grant said.

"Exactly. Sand Island," Christina replied.

"Then, that's where we're going!" Grant whispered.

16
HIDE AND SEEK, GHOST STYLE

"Let's go!" Christina said. She tugged the hood of Grant's sweatshirt.

The ferryboat going to Sand Island was leaving, and Christina wanted to make sure that she and Grant were on it.

"Alright, already!" Grant said, stumbling back as Christina yanked him.

Christina and Grant boarded the ferry. They were the last, and seemingly only ones, on the ferry. The metal door slammed shut, and the engines of the boat roared to life.

Christina peered out onto Lake Superior and saw dark clouds gathering.

DING! DING! Christina thrust her hand into her pocket and yanked out the phone. It flew from her grasp and skittered along the floor of the boat.

Grant dove after it, sliding on the wooden deck on his knees. The ferry listed left then right with the swell of the waves.

"Get it, Grant!" Christina yelled. "I need it to keep in touch with Mimi!"

"Trying to!" he grunted, reaching under the bench seat where the phone had lodged itself.

"Got it!" Grant yelled and sat up, bumping his head on the wooden bench.

"YEOW!" he howled.

Grant stumbled and wove his way back to Christina. The rising waves rocked the shuttle boat.

"Hurry, we're almost there!" Grant said. He noticed that the island was rapidly approaching.

"Okay," Christina flipped the phone open. Her fingers trembled.

YOU'RE ON YOUR WAY TO
COME AND PLAY. DARE YOU TO
FIND ME IN MY RED AND WHITE
GRAVE.

The wind picked up, creating a howling sound.

Christina flicked the phone shut. "We need to do this quickly."

"Okay. We'll need to look for something red and white," Grant said.

"Shouldn't be too hard," Christina said. "It doesn't look like there's much of anything out there."

Grant spun around. Their island destination looked like mostly trees. But there was something sticking up and out from the tree line.

"A house with a lighthouse!" Christina yelled.

Grant jumped. "Of course! That's all there is out here."

Christina nodded. "Now all we have to do is get off this boat."

17
RED AND WHITE, UP OR DOWN

Black clouds blanketed the sky. Christina and Grant scampered off the shuttle boat. A light rain began to fall.

"Hurry!" Christina yelled.

"I AM!" Grant shouted back.

As they ran, Christina looked up, guiding their direction. She could see a lighthouse made of brick.

They bolted out of the woods and onto a lush green lawn. There sat a small, one-story brick house with an octagonal lighthouse attached.

"The entrance is over here!" Grant yelled.

"But that's the entrance to the house!" Christina cried.

"I don't see any other entrance," Grant explained. He tried the handle. The door creaked opened! "Over here, Christina.

Grant stepped in and Christina followed.

A flash of lightning lit up the sky, illuminating the small hallway. Christina stifled a scream.

A face!

"Grant! Someone is in here!" Christina said.

Grant reached for a lamp on a side table and switched it on. The room barely lit up.

"Christina?" Grant said. He turned to face her. Christina was looking intently at something on the wall. He joined her. An array of pictures smiled back at them.

"It was just this portrait on the wall. Grant, isn't that the hotel guy?" Christina said.

"You're right! He lives here?" asked Grant.

"Take a look at this," Christina said, pointing to a framed newspaper clipping. "Here he's with the governor. He's receiving some sort of award, and...wait...this is Ichabod?"

"What? Mr. Icky?" asked Grant.

"That's what the article says. So, Ichabod has been sending those messages! This is THE lighthouse! We have to warn Mimi and Papa!" shouted Christina.

"Your phone!" Grant said.

Christina fumbled in her pocket and pulled out her cell phone. She quickly pressed the speed dial for Mimi. She waited for Mimi to pick up.

"She's not picking up, Grant." Then, "Oh, hello, Mimi, is that you? Mimi, Grant and I are at Ichabod's lighthouse. Mimi? Mimi, are you there?" Christina turned to her brother and said, "Grant, we were cut off!"

"Let's go, then!" Grant suggested.

They tried the door. It was locked from the outside! They peered outside and saw a man with a crooked smile quickly walk by.

"It's Ichabod!" Grant shouted. "He locked us in!"

"Quick, turn off the light!" Christina commanded.

Grant and Christina stood for just a few moments, allowing their eyes to adjust.

"There are stairs that go down over here," Grant said.

Christina looked around. It appeared that the stairs were their only option. "Okay, let's go."

"You go first," Grant said, nudging Christina forward.

"Okay, follow me," Christina said.

Grant was not as cautious, and lost his footing. His feet kicked up and he slipped.

"Whoa!" Grant yelled.

"Careful," Christina said. "We're almost there. I can see a small light ahead."

Grant followed Christina to the end of the stairway and into a damp, musty room.

"It's the basement," Grant noted.

Christina looked around. The dimly lit room had antique furniture in one corner and a pile of wood in another.

RUMMMMBLE! Thunder echoed down the stairs.

Grant looked at Christina. "Now what?"

"We need to find a way out, or up," she said.

Christina squinted and noticed a splintery wooden door in the opposite corner of the basement. She crossed the room and opened it. Inside was a black iron, spiral stairwell. "It goes up," she said. "These must be to the lighthouse. Maybe I'll have better reception up there. I could try Mimi again."

Grant said, "Ladies first."

"Gee, thanks," Christina said sarcastically.

Christina held onto the black iron rail and started ascending the stairs. It was a very tight stairwell with not much room to move. She tripped going up, and Grant nearly fell over her. She grabbed her knee, stifling a scream, and sat upright. Just then, the heel of her foot scraped up against something. She reached down and felt around with her hand. "A speaker? What would a speaker be doing on the stairwell and down this low?" she asked Grant.

"I don't know, but let's keep going," urged Grant.

Up and up they climbed, around and around the tower steps. A tiny sliver of light from the top of the lighthouse guided their way.

Suddenly, a bright light burst into their dark quarters. Lightning...again!

"EEIIIEE!" Grant screamed.

A loud rumble of thunder echoed in the tiny round chamber.

Christina slowed her approach toward the top.

With just a few steps to go, Christina stopped. She swallowed hard and took the last step. Grant followed.

When both kids reached the top, six lights suddenly popped on! And in those lights were six scary faces!

18
CREEPY FACES IN CREEPY PLACES

"AAAAHHHHH!" Christina screamed.

"AAAAHHHHH!" Grant screamed and grabbed his sister.

"SURPRISE!" the six faces shouted.

Christina looked closely once she recovered from the fright. The lights were flashlights and the faces were familiar. It was Mimi, Papa, and four other people. They held a lighthouse-shaped cake with red frosting words, Happy Birthday, Christina!

"Happy Birthday, Christina!" they all shouted in unison.

Christina didn't know whether to be elated, furious, or scared, because she felt all those feelings at once.

"Nicole, Dominic, you're here, too?" Christina asked. She saw a woman with curly black hair. She wasn't wearing her nametag, but Christina remembered her from the store.

"This is Susan, Ichabod's daughter," Mimi explained. "She was in on the surprise, too. She even made your birthday cake for you."

Christina managed a tight thank you and a smile. But there were more pressing matters.

"We called to warn you!" Christina shot a hard glance at Mr. Ichabod and pointed at him. "He's been sending mysterious text messages that led us here. He locked us in the main house just now. We had to escape!"

"Papa, Mr. Ichabod is not who you think he is!" Grant warned.

"And if Ichabod works at the hotel, why did we have to come all the way over here to meet him?" Christina implored.

Mr. Ichabod inched closer to the door.

"The hotel? Ichabod doesn't work at the hotel, Christina," Mimi explained.

The door slammed shut.

"Ichabod's gone!" yelled Grant. "He's getting away!"

They tried the door. It was locked! But suddenly, they heard footsteps coming up the stairs. The door creaked open. There, standing in the doorway, were two Ichabods! One was holding the other forcibly by the arm.

"Christina, Grant, I want to apologize for my brother, Walter. When you mentioned the hotel, I knew in an instant who it was. Walter owns the hotel you stayed at. I had to catch him before he escaped," Ichabod explained.

"I," Christina began, "I didn't know."

"You have a twin?" Mimi asked, surprised.

"I do," Ichabod replied. "We haven't gotten along since our parents died over two decades ago."

"What will happen now?" Grant asked.

"How about telling us why!" Christina ventured. "Why would you go around scaring kids like that?"

Walter wore the look of defeat all over his face. Even his body, all bent over, looked nothing like the confident man at the hotel.

He didn't say a word until Papa took a step toward him.

Obviously intimidated, Walter looked at Christina and then back at his twin brother.

"I've wanted this lighthouse ever since Dad and Mom left it to you in the will," Walter said. "This place could make so much money! You don't even charge admission! If I had this place, I would turn it into a real goldmine!"

"But, what does that have to do with scaring kids?" Grant asked accusingly.

Walter was quiet again.

"You knew we were coming into town when we made the reservation, didn't you?" Mimi asked.

"But how did he get *my* cell number?" Christina asked. "Oh, I know—Mimi, you had to use my phone to call the hotel! You couldn't find yours!"

Christina put her hands on her hips and looked at Walter. "I'll bet you made those ghost sounds! I found your hidden speaker in the stairwell."

Even Ichabod looked sternly at his brother. Walter nodded and stared at the floor.

"I've figured it out!" Christina said, looking at Walter. "You were trying to take over the lighthouse! You thought you could scare your brother away from his home by making him think it was haunted! And to make sure he'd leave, you went around pretending to be him and scaring us kids. That would make him look real bad, and he'd be forced out by the community! Then, you'd have the hotel *and* the lighthouse all to yourself!"

Walter nodded. "You're right," he admitted. "Ichabod, I'm sorry! I know how much this place means to you. But I also knew you'd never let me near it."

"Why didn't you just ask?" Ichabod said. "I really wouldn't mind a change of scenery— and I wouldn't mind having my brother back."

"Really? Just like that?" asked Walter.

"We're too old to hold onto grudges," Ichabod replied. "And besides, we can be partners, with the hotel too."

"Kids, I'm sorry I frightened you," began Walter. "I must admit, I was really impressed with your sleuthing abilities. You get that from your grandmother."

"Well, Christina," said Mimi, "so what do you think of your surprise birthday so far?" For once, Christina was at a loss for words. Everyone laughed.

"Oh, by the way, why didn't you tell ME about the surprise party?" asked Grant.

"Because we had to keep it a SECRET!" Papa replied, rubbing his knuckles in Grant's sweaty blond hair. "So, what are we waiting for? Let's have some cake!"

Papa and Ichabod cut the cake and passed out huge hunks to everyone. Even Walter devoured a piece or two.

"Mimi, no wonder you didn't put up a fuss when we asked to come over to the island—alone! You knew we'd make our way over here. You knew we couldn't help ourselves!" Christina said through a mouthful of yummy birthday cake.

"Yeah," Grant added, "even after almost getting swallowed whole by a giant cave!"

Mimi and Papa laughed. Mimi said, "Well, you two are certainly curious! That's for certain!"

Grant and Dominic took off running to explore the lighthouse, but not before grabbing another piece of cake.

"Well, thank you all," Christina said, looking at Mimi and Papa, then at her new friends. "This really IS the best birthday ever!"

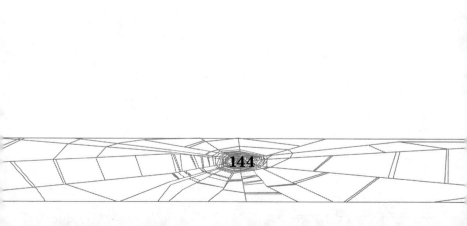

144

19
GREAT LAKES GOODBYES

Grant, Christina, Mimi, and Papa stood out on the front lawn of the brick lighthouse. Their friends had all gone back home—for real this time. The blazing morning sun glistened on the calm, peaceful waters of Lake Superior.

"Thanks for letting us stay here last night," Papa said to Mr. Ichabod.

"No trouble at all. It's always nice to have friends come to stay. You know, we don't get many visitors out here," Mr. Ichabod said. Then, he added, "We might see that change with Walter as a partner."

"Mimi and Papa, not only was this the best birthday ever, but I really had a great time on the Great Lakes!" Christina said. "I never knew that the lakes were so beautiful and had so much cool history!"

"Glad you had a good time, Christina," Mimi said.

"Not only that—we solved a mystery," said Christina.

"And don't forget—we brought two brothers back together!" added Grant.

"Well, I don't know about you all, but I had the darnedest time falling asleep last night. Did no one but me hear the shuffling of footsteps in the night?" Papa asked.

"These lighthouses are centuries old. There's bound to be a ghost or two roaming the stairwells," Mimi replied.

Grant and Christina looked at each other and smiled slyly. They knew the value of a good prank.

"Well, maybe some mysteries just defy explanation?" Christina suggested.

"Or maybe they just get figured out later?" said Mimi.

"I guess that means we'll have to come back!" said Papa merrily.

Christina and Grant exchanged glances.

"WE DON'T THIIIINK SOOOOOO!" they shouted.

Well, that was fun!

Wow, glad we solved that mystery!

Where shall we go next?

EVERYWHERE!

The End

What I Did on My Vacation
by Christina

My brother Grant and I, and my Mimi and Papa took a fun and somewhat scary vacation to the Great Lakes. I was surprised at how large they are, how important they are to the shipping industry, and how treacherous they can be, especially during winter storms called nor'easters. As usual, we were involved in a mystery.

(I mean, I know you have read my vacation reports before!) But this time, it was different; part of the mystery was downright scary, but part was, well, I just don't quite know what it was—so, I guess that makes it still a mystery to me!

Now...go to
www.carolemarshmysteries.com
and...

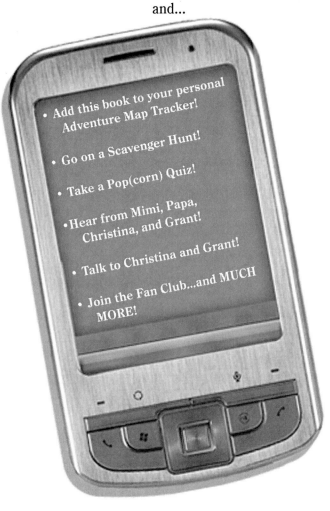

- Add this book to your personal Adventure Map Tracker!

- Go on a Scavenger Hunt!

- Take a Pop(corn) Quiz!

- Hear from Mimi, Papa, Christina, and Grant!

- Talk to Christina and Grant!

- Join the Fan Club...and MUCH MORE!

SAT GLOSSARY

intrigue: to cause interest, to make curious

collapse: to break or fall down

foliage: leaves of a tree or plant

maneuver: to get around difficult obstacles

nuisance: something that annoys or irritates

GLOSSARY

Great Lakes: five large lakes in the northern United States and Canada

lighthouse: a structure that lights up coastal areas so ships will not crash onto shore

maritime: having to do with the water or sea

nor'easter: a strong storm that blows in from the northeast; also known as northeaster

peninsula: a strip of land surrounded by water on three sides

pollution: debris, trash, or contaminants that make a place unfit or dangerous for people and animals to live there

sand dune: large mound of sand formed by wind or water

THE MYSTERY

AT

Fort Sumter

1
"WHAT FORT IS THIS?"

GRANT yawned. When the car stopped, he looked up to see that they were parked in front of what looked like a grand fortress.

"Are we going to sleep at Fort Sumter?" he asked, yawning again. He turned off his video player, thrusting the car from green gloom to just plain old black gloom.

"This is not Fort Sumter," said Papa, stretching, his cowboy hat scraping the roof. "This is a hotel. It's the old Citadel building, and yes, the young men who once stayed here would say it is indeed a fortress." Papa laughed.

From the back seat, Christina and Grant stared at the edifice shrouded in fogged light, then stared at each other. They shrugged their shoulders.

"Looks like a fort to me," Christina whispered to her brother.

"Towers...turrets...gun ports..." said Grant. "Yep, looks like a fort to me."

A GIANT yawn escaped from the front seat. "Are we sleeping at Fort Sumter?!" cried Mimi.

She stretched and sat straight up, her short blond hair a spiky mess.

"Oh, for gosh sakes!" moaned Papa. "It's a hotel! Or, we can sleep in the car."

"Uh, no thanks!" said Christina, shoving the Clemson afghan aside. She gathered her things. "There is no bathroom in the car."

"Or television," reminded Grant, eagerly grabbing his backpack.

Papa opened the car door as a sleepy bellman in a uniform approached. "No TV. It's late. It's bedtime. Let's go, pard'ners—NOW!"

The kids, and even Mimi, "hopped to."

"Wow," Christina whispered to her brother. "Papa sounds like a drill sergeant or something."

"He's just tired," said Mimi. "That drive in the sleet on the dark road is nerve-wracking."

"Mimi!" said Grant. "You were asleep...how do you know?"

Mimi turned around. Her eyes were still red from weeping over poor Aunt Lulu. "Now, Grant, you know how I have eyes in the back of my head?"

"Yes, ma'am," Grant said.

"Well, guess what?" said Mimi. "I can also 'backseat drive' your Papa from the front seat—even with my eyes closed."

Papa, who was holding her door open, shook his head. "It's true, Grant, and don't forget it. You can't get anything past Mimi." He gave Mimi a weary wink.

Mimi smiled and perked up. She hopped out of the car and followed the bellman and their luggage cart inside. Papa, Christina, and Grant followed obediently.

"Well, do we even get dinner?" Grant asked forlornly. He rubbed his tummy and tried to look like a starving waif. He and his sister waited eagerly for the answer.

Mimi and Papa barely turned their heads around, but together they said, "NO!"

As Christina entered the spooky, fortlike hotel, she noted the time on the lobby clock.

"Forgetaboutit, Grant," she said sadly, putting her arm around her brother's shoulders. "It's closer to breakfast than dinnertime. I have some M&Ms in my backpack. We'll make do."

"Great!" grumbled Grant. "Next, I guess we'll find out we're staying in the dungeon?"

Papa hovered over the check-in desk. A skeletal-looking desk clerk handed him a key. "The room you requested, sir," they overheard him say. "The Dungeon Suite."

Christina and Grant exchanged shocked glances, and nervously followed their grandparents into the gloom of the darkened lobby.